The
Elephant's
Child

Retold by Robert James

Illustrated by Garyfallia Leftheri

FRANKLIN WATTS
LONDON•SYDNEY

First published in 2010 by
Franklin Watts
338 Euston Road
London
NW1 3BH

Franklin Watts Australia
Level 17/207 Kent Street
Sydney
NSW 2000

A CIP catalogue record for this book is available
from the British Library.

ISBN 978 0 7496 9408 1 (hbk)
ISBN 978 0 7496 9414 2 (pbk)

Series Editor: Jackie Hamley
Series Advisor: Catherine Glavina
Series Designer: Peter Scoulding

Printed in China

Franklin Watts is a division of
Hachette Children's Books,
an Hachette UK company.
www.hachette.co.uk

This Just So story is
based on a tale written
by an author called
Rudyard Kipling over
a hundred years ago.

Just So stories give fun
ideas for why different
animals are like they are.

Long ago, Elephant
had a short nose.

3

The Elephant's child
was always asking
questions.

Why? What?

Who? How?

One day, he asked,
"What does Crocodile
eat for dinner?"

Nobody would tell him.

So the Elephant's
child asked a bird.

"Go to the river and find out!" replied the bird.

There, the Elephant's
child saw an animal
like a log.

11

"Are you Crocodile?"
he asked.

"Yes!" said Crocodile.

"What do you eat for dinner?" asked the Elephant's child.

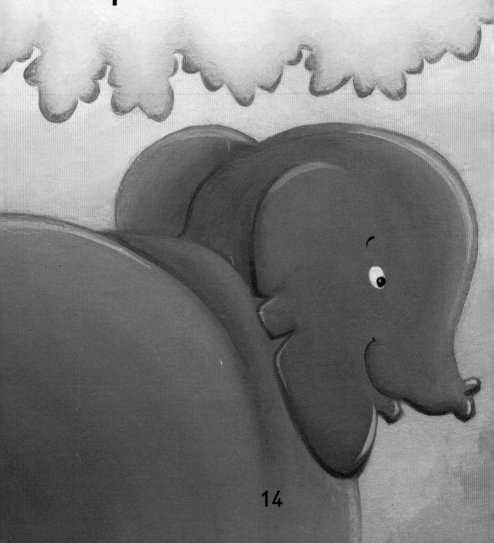

14

"Come closer and I'll tell you," smiled Crocodile.

Crocodile bit the
Elephant child's
short nose.

"Help!" cried the Elephant's child.

The Elephant's child
pulled and pulled.

His nose got longer
and longer.

And that is how
Elephant got his
long nose!

Puzzle Time!

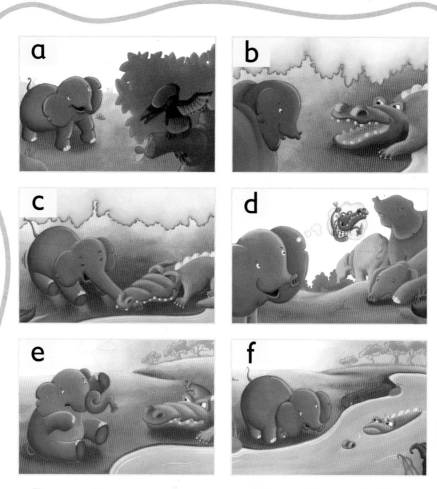

Put these pictures in the right order and tell the story!

curious

sly

nosy

cunning

Which words describe the
Elephant's child and which
describe Crocodile?

Turn over for answers!

Notes for adults

TADPOLES are structured to provide support for newly independent readers. The stories may also be used by adults for sharing with young children.

Starting to read alone can be daunting. **TADPOLES** help by providing visual support and repeating words and phrases. These books will both develop confidence and encourage reading and rereading for pleasure.

If you are reading this book with a child, here are a few suggestions:

1. Make reading fun! Choose a time to read when you and the child are relaxed and have time to share the story.
2. Talk about the story before you start reading. Look at the cover and the blurb. What might the story be about? Why might the child like it?
3. Encourage the child to retell the story, using the jumbled picture puzzle as a starting point. Extend vocabulary with the matching words to characters puzzle.
4. Talk about how the story has fun with how different animals look, and see if you can think of other animals and why they might look the way they do.
5. Give praise! Remember that small mistakes need not always be corrected.

Answers

Here is the correct order:

1. d 2. a 3. f 4. b 5. c 6. e

Words to describe the Elephant's child:
curious, nosy

Words to describe Crocodile:
cunning, sly